ELI MANNING

Pete DiPrimio

Mitchell Lane
PUBLISHERS

P.O. Box 196
Hockessin, Delaware 19707
Visit us on the web: www.mitchelllane.com
Comments? email us: mitchelllane@mitchelllane.com

Mitchell Lane **PUBLISHERS**

Printing   2   3   4   5   6   7   8   9

A Robbie Reader
Contemporary Biography

Library of Congress Cataloging-in-Publication Data
DiPrimio, Pete.
  Eli Manning / by Pete DiPrimio.
     p. cm. — (A Robbie Reader)
  Includes bibliographical references and index.
  ISBN 978-1-58415-726-7 (library bound)
  1. Manning, Eli, 1981– —Juvenile literature. 2. Football players—United States—Biography—Juvenile literature. I. Title.
  GV939.M289D57 2008
  796.332092—dc22
  [B]
                                                                            2008020893

ABOUT THE AUTHOR: Pete DiPrimio is a veteran sports columnist for the *Fort Wayne [Indiana] News-Sentinel*, a long-time freelance feature, fiction, and travel writer. He is the author of three nonfiction books pertaining to Indiana University athletics and of *Tom Brady* for Mitchell Lane Publishers.

PHOTO CREDITS: Cover, pp. 1, 3—Ben Liebenberg/NFL Photos/Getty Images; pp. 4, 11—Paul Spinelli/Getty Images; p. 6—Evan Pinkus/Getty Images; p. 9—Drew Hallowell/Getty Images; p. 12—Blake Sims/Allsport/Getty Images; p. 16—Matthew Stockman/Getty Images; p. 18—AP Photo/Scott Audette; p. 19—Chris Trotman/Getty Images; p. 20—David Drapkin/Getty Images; pp. 22, 27—AP Photo/Cheryl Gerber; p. 24—AP Photo/Bebeto Matthews.

TABLE OF CONTENTS

Words in **bold** type can be found in the glossary.

New York quarterback Eli Manning (#10) avoids getting sacked by New England defensive players during Super Bowl XLII. Manning led the Giants to a 17-14 upset of the previously undefeated Patriots.

Super Ending

Eli Manning had no time to doubt or listen to those who doubted him. He knew what he could do as the New York Giants **quarterback**, and now he had the world's largest football stage—the 2008 **Super Bowl** in Phoenix, Arizona—to prove it.

A year earlier New York fans had blamed Eli for the team's losing seven of its last nine games. They said he wasn't tough enough and wasn't as good as older brother Peyton, the superstar quarterback for the Indianapolis Colts. Retired Giants running back Tiki Barber, who had become an NBC TV broadcaster, said before the 2007 season that Eli was a bad leader.

These comments bothered Eli, but he didn't say much about it publicly. He'd let his

In 2008, Eli Manning (#10) made big plays with his legs as well as his arm to lead New York over New England in one of the biggest upsets in Super Bowl history.

playing speak for him—and it did. In playoff wins over Tampa Bay, Dallas, and Green Bay, Eli completed 53 of 85 passes for 599 yards, four touchdowns, and no **interceptions**.

In Super Bowl XLII, New York faced 18-0 New England. The Patriots were 13½-point favorites. They had already beaten New York 38-35 in the regular season finale. They were trying to become only the second team in the 42-year Super Bowl era to go undefeated. (The 1972 Miami Dolphins were the first.)

Then there was the *Sports Illustrated* jinx, which said that any person or team that appeared on the magazine's cover would lose. Eli had appeared on the cover of the January 28, 2008, issue after leading New York over Green Bay. It hit the stands just over a week before the Super Bowl.

The Giants led 10-7 with eight minutes left in the game. They had the ball and were driving to finish off New England. Eli scrambled and overthrew a wide-open pass to Plaxico Burress that might have led to a victory-clinching **touchdown**. Some fans booed. Same old Eli, they said.

New England got the ball back and scored to make it 14-10 with 2:42 left. The Giants, and Eli, would have one more chance. But a three-point field goal wouldn't work. They had to go 83 yards for a touchdown.

The key play came on the third down near midfield. Eli went back to pass. The Patriots swarmed him. Defensive lineman Jarvis Green grabbed Eli's jersey. **Linebacker** Adalius Thomas and defensive lineman Richard Seymour surrounded him. Somehow, Eli pulled free and saw receiver David Tyree deep down the middle. Eli threw it high and far.

The pass seemed too high and New England linebacker Rodney Harrison had Tyree covered. But Tyree jumped as high as he could, higher than it seemed possible. He grabbed the ball, trapped it against his helmet, and fought Harrison all the way to the ground. In practice two days earlier, Tyree had dropped six passes. This time he refused to let go. The 32-yard catch put New York 21 yards away from the **end zone**.

"It was an unbelievable catch," Eli said.

"I don't know if there's been a bigger play in the Super Bowl," New York coach Tom Coughlin said.

But the game wasn't won yet.

The Giants reached the 13-yard line with 39 seconds left. Burress lined up outside with

Eli Manning (#10) not only avoided a sack on this fourth-quarter play, he completed a key 32-yard pass that set up the Giants' winning touchdown.

only cornerback Ellis Hobbs to cover him because the Patriots were sending everybody else after Eli. Burress is 6-foot-5 and 232 pounds. Hobbs is 5-foot-9 and 195. Burress faked inside then cut outside. Hobbs went for the fake and Burress was wide open. Eli tossed him the ball and New York had the lead and the victory, 17-14. It was the second-biggest upset in NFL Super Bowl history behind the New York Jets beating Baltimore in 1969.

Grumpy New England coach Bill Belichick left the field before the clock reached zero. "They made some plays," he said. "We made some plays. They just made a few more."

In the fourth quarter, with everything on the line, Eli completed 8 of 12 passes for 143 yards and two touchdowns. He finished 19-for-34 for 255 yards.

Eli talked about how much it meant to him, to the team, and to New York fans. "To win, not just for me, but for our whole team, is really special. For me personally, it is kind of sweet."

The Giants celebrated at their Phoenix hotel. Eli was there with his mother, Olivia, and

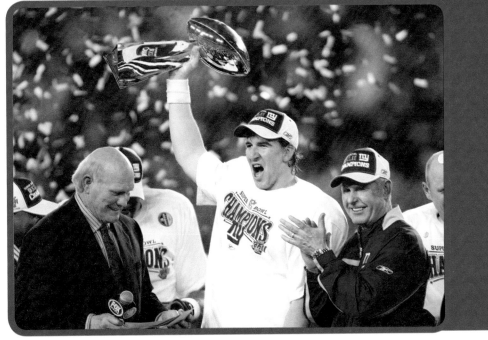

Eli Manning shows off the Vince Lombardi Trophy that goes to the Super Bowl winner. The victory silenced a lot of doubters who wondered if Manning could ever win a big game.

fiancée, Abby McGrew. His older brothers, Cooper and Peyton, were also there. So were friends from Mississippi, his college, and from Isidore Newman, his New Orleans high school. Eli and Cooper even sang the song "New York, New York."

Eli had always played in Peyton's shadow. Not anymore. Peyton needed nine years to win a Super Bowl with the Colts. Eli did it in four.

Nobody doubts him now.

Eli was one of the best college quarterbacks in America while playing for the University of Mississippi.

Early Years

Elisha Nelson Manning was born on January 3, 1981, in New Orleans, Louisiana. His parents, Archie and Olivia, already had two sons—Cooper and Peyton. Archie was an NFL quarterback and **public speaker** who had been an outstanding player at the University of Mississippi. Olivia, the Mississippi Homecoming Queen as a college senior, was a stay-at-home mom. They lived in a very nice neighborhood—the Garden District—in New Orleans.

All three brothers were born to be football players. They would play games in the backyard—tackle football, not touch. They would dress in full uniforms with helmets and pads. They would even sing the national anthem before playing.

Cooper, the oldest, was a very good high school wide receiver who signed with Mississippi. Then, in 1992, a bulging disc in his neck ended his playing career.

Peyton was a great high school quarterback (Cooper caught many of his passes) and then a National Player of the Year Candidate at Tennessee. He was the NFL's number one pick in 1998 by the Indianapolis Colts. He won MVP honors in 2003, then led the Colts to the 2007 Super Bowl title.

Eli is five years younger than Peyton and seven years younger than Cooper. Eli was quiet (he didn't start talking until he was three). Peyton would often pick on Eli. He would pin him to the ground, then hit Eli until he could name all the teams in the Southeastern **Conference**. That conference has schools such as Alabama, Florida, Mississippi, and Tennessee. Cooper would often have to rescue Eli.

While Eli was growing up, Archie traveled a lot to give speeches, and Cooper and Peyton would spend time with their friends. Eli and his mom would do a lot of activities together, like go to movies. Olivia was calm when things went wrong, and Eli acted like her. That's how he got the nickname Easy.

By the time Eli got to Isidore Newman High School, everybody knew he would be a very good quarterback. As a **sophomore** (SOF-moor), he threw for 2,340 yards and 24 touchdowns. As a junior he led Newman to a 9-1 record and the state **playoffs**. Every major college in the country wanted him.

In his senior year, Eli led Newman to an 11-1 record. He finished his high school career with 81 touchdowns and 7,389 passing yards, 200 more yards than Peyton. Now he had a big decision to make. Mississippi, his father's school, really wanted him. So did Tennessee, where Peyton had gone. After a lot of thinking, Eli chose Mississippi.

Eli Manning had a lot of success at Mississippi. He led the Rebels to a 24-13 record during his three seasons as starting quarterback. He also met his future wife, Abby McGrew, in college.

A Time to Grow

Eli didn't play his first year because Mississippi had more experienced quarterbacks. He became the starter as a sophomore. The Rebels went 7-4 in 2001. Eli threw for 31 touchdowns and set or tied 17 school records. The next year they were 7-6 and beat Nebraska in the Independence Bowl. Eli threw for 3,401 yards and 21 touchdowns. He thought about leaving college to enter the **NFL Draft**. Instead, he came back for the 2003 season and led Mississippi to a 10-3 record. He threw for 3,600 yards and 29 touchdowns. He won the Maxwell Award as the nation's best player (Peyton had won the same award in 1997) and the Southeastern Conference Player of the Year. For his career he had thrown for 10,119 yards, 81 touchdowns, and 35 interceptions.

Eli holds the Maxwell Trophy, which is given every year to college football's best all-around player. He won the award in 2003 after leading Mississippi to a 10-3 record.

Eli was ready for the NFL, but there was a problem. The San Diego Chargers, who had the first pick in the draft, wanted Eli, but Archie was afraid the Chargers were a bad team. He had never had a winning record during his 14-year NFL career and he didn't want that for Eli. So the Mannings told San Diego not to pick him.

Eli celebrates joining the New York Giants along with brother Peyton, Peyton's wife Ashley, mother Olivia, future wife Abby McGrew, and father Archie.

On draft day San Diego made Eli the number one pick anyway. He said he would not play for San Diego. He said he would go to law school. Then the Chargers traded Eli to New York for quarterback Philip Rivers and a draft pick that eventually became All-Pro linebacker Shawne Merriman. Some experts said New York had made a mistake. Eli didn't care. He was very happy. He was even happier when he signed a six-year, $45 million contract.

As a rookie in the NFL, Eli struggled. He lost his first four games, threw too many interceptions, and finished with a 1-6 record as a first-year starter.

New York Struggles

As a rookie, Eli had to earn the starting quarterback job. The Giants already had veteran quarterback Kerry Collins. They had also signed another quarterback, former NFL Most Valuable Player Kurt Warner.

Eli was nervous at the team's first **mini-camp** in May. He missed receivers and fumbled snaps. Nobody said being an NFL quarterback would be easy.

In his first game, he completed 17 of 37 passes for 162 yards. He threw one touchdown and two interceptions. The Giants lost to Atlanta, 14-10.

Eli played terribly in his next three games— all losses. Against Baltimore he completed only four passes for 27 yards. He played better in a loss to Pittsburgh, then led New York to a 28-24 win over Dallas—the first victory of his pro career. He did it by directing a game-winning drive late in the fourth quarter.

It was a sign of things to come.

After a 1-6 rookie record, he and the Giants kept improving, although not fast

Peyton, Eli, and Archie Manning know a good quarterback when they see one. They gave Southern California's Matt Leinart (second from left) the Manning Award for outstanding quarterback play in 2005. The award goes to the nation's top college quarterback.

enough for some people. They made the playoffs the next two years, but lost their first game both times. Fans weren't happy. They said mean things about Eli when New York opened the 2007 season 0-2. He ignored that and the newspaper and website writers who wondered if he'd ever be good enough.

Then the Giants started winning. They made the playoffs again and beat Tampa Bay and Dallas. They advanced to the NFC title game at Green Bay. While Eli was in town, a Green Bay TV station refused to broadcast *Seinfeld* the day before the game because programmers knew *Seinfeld* was Eli's favorite TV show. Easy Eli wasn't bothered by the prank.

On a freezing night in Green Bay, Eli was a star. He ignored the minus-1-degree temperature and minus-23-degree wind chill. He completed 21 of 40 passes for 254 yards, and New York beat the favored Packers 23-20. After that, receiver Plaxico Burress called Eli "the captain of our ship." That captain was leading the Giants to the Super Bowl.

Eli accepts thirteen-year-old Roy Santiago's pushup challenge as part of an exercise program put on by the NFL and the American Heart Association. Eli is very involved in charities and fitness programs.

Role Model

Eli's Super Bowl success will make him very wealthy off the field, although probably not as wealthy as his brother. Peyton makes $13 million a year by doing commercials for such companies as MasterCard, DirecTV, and Gatorade. No other NFL player makes more.

By 2008, Eli was already making about $5 million a year from companies such as Nabisco, Citizen Watch, and Reebok. He also did a funny ESPN Sportscenter commercial that included his mother and father and Peyton. In the commercial, he and Peyton are hitting each other during a tour of the ESPN studio.

Some experts think Eli could make another $5 million a year, for a total of $10 million, if he accepts all the offers he will get. Why? He is very popular. For instance, his No. 10 jersey climbed from 20th in sales on December 31, 2007, to number 8 on January 26, 2008.

On April 19, 2008, Eli married his college sweetheart, Abby McGrew, at a resort in Mexico. The ceremony was held on a beach by the Sea of Cortez. It was private, attended by 60 friends and family members.

Eli is very involved with charities in the New York area. He and Peyton organized and joined in airlifts of emergency supplies to New Orleans victims after Hurricane Katrina hit the city in August of 2005. He gave money to Habitat for Humanity International's Katrina Relief Fund. He has joined in many **fund-raising** events.

Still, most people will remember him for football. New York assistant coach Kevin Gilbride said Eli is not an overnight sensation, that he's successful because of how hard he's worked. Some people criticized Eli's lack of fire, but he's always been calm. He said he treats praise and criticism the same way—he ignores them.

Eli helped with the cleanup of New Orleans after Hurricane Katrina damaged much of the city in 2005. He was part of the Katrina Krewe.

"That stuff doesn't make a difference," he said. "It doesn't change what you're going to do next week."

Eli won't change. He will focus on what *does* make a difference. That's what matters in the end.

27

CAREER STATS

Year	Team	G	GS	Comp	Att	Pct	Yards	YPA	Lg	TD	Int	Rate
2004	NYG	9	7	95	197	48.2	1,043	5.3	52	6	9	55.4
2005	NYG	16	16	294	557	52.8	3,762	6.8	78	24	17	75.9
2006	NYG	16	16	301	522	57.7	3,244	6.2	55	24	18	77.0
2007	NYG	16	16	297	529	56.1	3,336	6.3	60	23	20	73.9
Total		57	55	987	1,805	54.7	11,385	6.3	78	77	64	73.4

(G=Games, GS=Games started, Comp=Completions, Att=Attempts, Pct=Percentage, YPA=Yards per attempt, Lg=Longest pass, TD=Touchdown, Int=Interceptions, Rate=Quarterback rating)

CHRONOLOGY

1981   Elisha Nelson Manning is born on January 3 in New Orleans.

2000   After graduating from Isidore Newman High School in New Orleans, he picks the University of Mississippi over the University of Tennessee.

2001   In his first year as a college starter, Eli throws for 31 touchdowns and nine interceptions; Mississippi goes 7-4.

2002   He throws for 3,401 yards and 21 touchdowns. Mississippi goes 7-6 and beats Nebraska in the Independence Bowl.

2003   Eli is honored as a Maxwell Award Winner and SEC Player of the Year; he leads the Rebels to a 10-3 record.

CHRONOLOGY

2004   He is the NFL's number one pick by San Diego but is traded to New York. He goes 1-6 as a rookie starter.

2005   Eli guides the New York Giants to an 11-5 record and to the playoffs. They lose the first playoff game.

2006   Eli leads the Giants to the playoffs again, and another first-round loss.

2007   He leads New York to the playoffs for the third straight season and gets his first playoff win, against Tampa Bay. He also leads the Giants over favored Dallas and Green Bay.

2008   Eli leads the Giants over the New England Patriots, 17-14, one of the biggest upsets in NFL history. He is named Super Bowl MVP. Eli marries his longtime sweetheart, Abby McGrew, on April 19.

FIND OUT MORE

Books and Magazine Articles

Editors of *Sports Illustrated*. *Sports Illustrated, NY Giants Eli Manning*. January 28, 2008 (single-issue magazine).

Horn, Geoffrey M. *Peyton Manning*. Milwaukee: Garth Stevens Publishing, 2006.

Layden, Tim. "They're History." *Sports Illustrated*, February 11, 2008.

Mattern, Joanne. *Peyton Manning*. Hockessin, Delaware: Mitchell Lane Publishers, 2007.

Savage, Jeff. *Peyton Manning*. Minneapolis: Lerner Publishing Co., 2006.

Works Consulted

Peyton Manning Conference Call with Reporters, January 25, 2008.

"Eli Manning's Time Has Come," *CBS Sportsline*, February 4, 2008.

"Eli's Best Might Give Giants a Chance." *Indianapolis Star.* February 1, 2008.

FIND OUT MORE

"Former Giants GM Not Saying 'I Told You So'; Super Bowl Victory Gives Accorsi Vindication about Manning Trade." Associated Press, February 4, 2008. http://nbcsports.msnbc.com/id/22999758/

King, Peter. *Eli's The Manning: Surprise Star, Surprise Team. Sports Illustrated*, special issue. January 28, 2008.

Layden, Tim. "Hail Manning: Eli Is MVP—They're History." *Sports Illustrated Online*. February 6, 2008.

MacDonald, Brady. "Eli Manning to Disneyland: 'I'm Going to . . . the Bahamas.' " *Los Angeles Times*, February 7, 2008. http://travel.latimes.com/daily-deal-blog/?p=1311

Pells, Eddie. "Eli Manning Had to Escape a Huge Shadow to Find His Limelight." *Associated Press*, February 2, 2008. http://www.wsbt.com/sports/local/15150291.html

Skidmore, Sarah. "Super Bowl QBs Brady, Manning Offer Competing Marketability Off-Field." Associated Press. February 1, 2008. http://ww.uniontrib.com/sports/nfl/20080201-1142-superbowl-playermarketability.html

Vicarro, Mike. "Can You Say Upset? Don't Laugh: Giants Can Be Champs." *New York Post.* January 22, 2008.

Weisman, Larry. "Maturing Eli Is Proving to Be His Own Manning." *USA Today,* January 31, 2008. http://www.usatoday.com/sports/football/nfl/giants/2008-01-31-manning-cover_N.htm

Zimmerman, Paul. "Two-Minute Thrill." *Sports Illustrated Online*. February 5, 2008. http://sportsillustrated.cnn.com/2008/writers/dr_z/02/05/super.bowl0211/

On the Internet

NFL Player Profile: Eli Manning
http://www.nfl.com/players/elimanning/profile?id=MAN473170

New York Giants Official Website
http://www.giants.com

GLOSSARY

conference (KON-frents)—A grouping of teams. The NFL is divided into two 16-team conferences, the American Football Conference (AFC) and the National Football Conference (NFC).

end zone—Either end of the football field, where a team tries to take the ball to score.

fund-raising (FUND-ray-zing)—Events that will make money for people who need it, such as the poor or the hurt or the sick.

interception (in-ter-SEP-shun)—A pass caught by the opposing team.

linebacker (LYN-baa-kur)—A defensive player who is responsible for stopping the run as well as keeping receivers from catching the ball.

mini-camp—A three- or four-day training and workout camp for NFL teams, held in the spring. These camps help players get ready for the next season.

NFL—National Football League. The NFL is divided into two conferences, the American Football Conference (AFC) and the National Football Conference (NFC). The two best teams in each conference play for conference championships. The winners advance to the Super Bowl.

NFL Draft—The official choosing of players coming out of college, held every April by the 32 NFL teams.

playoffs—Games played between the best teams of the regular season; playoff winners go to the championship game.

public speaker—Somebody who talks in front of groups, often for pay.

quarterback (KWAR-ter-bak)—The player who runs the offense and throws the passes.

sacked (SAKT)—Knocked down the quarterback before he could throw the ball.

sophomore (SOF-moor)—Someone who is in the second year of experience.

Super Bowl—The NFL championship game. It matches the winners of the AFC and the NFC and is held on a Sunday in either late January or early February.

touchdown (TUTCH-down)—Moving the ball into the end zone to score. It is worth six points, and it earns the team a chance to win an extra (seventh) point.

INDEX